ANOTHER NIGHT ON
THE CITY STREETS
Stories from the Police Blotter

By

Patricia Rayzor Ditlevsen

CONTENTS

FORWARD

These short stories are roughly based on actual happenings during my career as a law enforcement officer. The names of all principals are fictitious, and any resemblance to real persons living or dead is entirely coincidental. I was one of the first sworn female law enforcement officers in Sacramento, CA. Of course, I've got a million stories to tell; these are just a few of them. I've always enjoyed creative writing. These stories are written in what is intended to be a T.V. series script format and narrated by the main character, Pat Salema. I hope you enjoy reading them as much as I enjoyed writing them.

CAST OF CHARACTERS

Pat Salema

Angel (Angelino Guadalupe Rojas y Martino Jones)

Michael McDoud

Robert Alexander Smythe

Mrs. Miriam Monahan

Kevin Watson

Jan Wyatt

Mitchell Morrissey

Rick Sullivan

CHAPTER ONE

POSSIBLE 261 IN-PROGRESS

"**F**our Charles six."

The dispatcher's voice intruded into what had been a comfortable lull in the conversation. Except for one or two "welfare checks," the radio had been silent through most of the night. We hadn't been swamped, and the shift was nearly two thirds over.

"Four Charles six, go ahead," my partner responded.

"Four Charles six; assault; possible 261 in progress; third and Main. Code three."

Four Charles six, en route. Any suspect descriptions?"

My partner's voice betrayed no emotion.

The dispatchers' reply was short, to the point, her voice almost dispassionate.

"No description. Female caller. No name. Reported woman screaming and scuffling sounds from the alley behind her apartment building. Too dark for her to see anything. A male voice yelling obscenities."

"Four Charles six, check."

To an onlooker these exchanges may have seemed too routine -- almost cold, but I could see the muscle along my partner's jaw tighten, and his fingers fumble slightly as he replaced the mic.

And how could anyone guess about the hard knot forming in the pit of my stomach and the staccato "thump-thump-thump" just under my breastbone? Was this just the result of the adrenalin rush that comes with a "hot" call?

I made a quick U-turn in midblock, activated the lights and siren and headed the unit south toward Main Street. My Mind kept repeating 261 ... rape. 261 ... rape. 261 ... rape.

I guided the black and white through the relatively light, midweek traffic without conscious effort, almost like a robot. We've been driving the same piece of junk for three months now. The Duty Sergeant keeps promising we'll get the next new one but he also said it sometimes rains in August around here. Get the picture?

I could feel the sweat between the steering wheel and the palms of my hands; those damnable numbers still drumming in my head: 261-261-261.

Scenes started popping out of my subconscious:

A woman standing in the middle of a room clutching her robe to her otherwise naked body.

A little boy sitting up suddenly in his bed crying out, "Mommy."

A hammer burying itself into a windowsill just inches from a hand, shattering the window glass.

Why can't I block out these memories? Won't they ever stop? It's always the same. Blood running icy cold, adrenalin surging like a flash flood, a momentary stab of raw fear, bitter gall rising in my mouth.

No matter how many times I hear that call, the reaction is the same: first the fear, then the hate. After all these years, still the hate.

"Hey, what the hell you trying to do, get us both killed?"

My partner's voice jerked me back to reality like a sharp slap across the face and I turned the wheel just in time to avoid driving straight through a detour sign and barrier.

I mumbled something obscene about construction crews who leave their tools lying around and a few minutes later I made the left turn onto Main Street.

Still frowning, my partner reached for the mic.

"Four Charles six."

"Four Charles six go ahead."

"Approaching third on Main. ETA about three minutes. We'll be out of the car."

"Four Charles six, check. Back up is one away."

Replacing the mic, my partner automatically reached for the shotgun lock and I killed the lights and siren.

"How the hell can you daydream at the wheel going code three to a hot call? My God, woman, I've been on the edge since we got this call. The thought of some son-of-a-bitch..."

I guess he must have seen something in my face just then because he never finished the sentence, and his voice softened with concern.

"You okay? Something wrong?"

"I'm okay. That was a close one. This stupid junk we have to drive won't turn smooth. Anyway, I didn't see the sign until I was almost on top of it. Maybe I need glasses."

He answered, "Yeah," but he sounded more than just a little skeptical. I could see him watching me out of the corner of his eye — my partner — always the worrier.

"My partner." Those are more than just words to me.

Angelino Guadalupe Rojas y Martino Jones (that's right, Jones) he is "Angel" to his friends, and every bit just that. Angel is the progeny of a Mexican born, very traditional, very Catholic mother and an American born Welsh father. The younger of his parents' two sons, he was raised on a recipe of love, hard work and good old fashion discipline (heavy on the love). His older brother is a prosecuting attorney. The two brothers are very close and Angel is fond of saying he became a cop to ensure his brother would never run short of customers.

Angel and I have been partners only one year but if ever a match was made in Heaven—pardon the pun.

He is ten years my junior, and I have at least that many years seniority over him but to listen to him, you'd think it was the other way around. Self-appointed bodyguard, father confessor and matchmaker, I refer to him as my "Guardian Angel." Sometimes, I swear he can read my mind. Close as we have been, however, I have never found the right moment to tell him my one deep secret.

I pulled the unit to the curb just as our back up unit pulled in behind us. As we approached the scene we could see we were not the first to arrive. A one-officer unit was parked at the curb near the alley in question. That unit, four Charles eight, had someone in the back seat behind the screen. It seems this officer was less than a half-block from the alley entrance when the call came over the air and had literally caught the assailant in the act.

The usual gallery of gawkers was hovering across the street or grouped on nearby porch steps. As we approached the alley, I could see brown hair barely visible above the seat of the other unit.

"He's a kid, just a punk kid, not more than eighteen or nineteen years old."

The voice speaking above the general din was at once incredulous and resigned. McDoud had seen it before but still couldn't accept it.

Michael McDoud had been a cop for fifteen of his forty-five years. Having come into the department almost directly from the military, he was fond of saying,

"I traded one war for another."

He's a good cop and a good husband who doesn't expect miracles. He wouldn't deny their existence either but he's an Irish Catholic who prefers to leave the miracle-making to the Almighty. Raised by an alcoholic widowed father, one would expect him to be bitter and sour on life. Quite the contrary. Somewhere around his third year in grade school, he met Alice O'Connor and fell helplessly in love. Her sweet nature and open disposition more than made up for whatever he may have missed at home. They married less than a year after graduating from high school. With "Allie" by his side, Michael was at peace with his life. He hasn't set out to save the world. He views his job as just that, a job but an honest one and he gives it an honest effort.

"Hey, McDoud, I see you got him," called out Angel.

"Yeah, the lousy punk," responded McDoud. "And her old enough to be his mother."

So saying, he gestured towards the other side of the alley entrance. Then still shaking his head and mumbling "the lousy punk," he took out his report book, leaned against the fender of his squad unit and started making notes.

Angel and I headed in the direction McDoud indicated. Another officer was attempting to speak to a figure cloaked in a blue blanket seated on the curb. A medic from the Fire Department ambulance was putting a dressing over the cut on her brow.

"That'll do for now but she should be seen at emergency. That cut may need stitches."

The medic packed up his gear and returned to his rig, and the figure retreated into the blanket once more.

As we approached, the officer looked up. It was a look of sheer frustration mixed with genuine concern. It was not the first time I had seen that look on the face of a brother officer. Most men, even trained law enforcement men, find it difficult to develop any kind of rapport with a rape victim. This officer was making little if any, progress in trying to interview this victim and it wasn't because he didn't care or try.

"Man, oh, man, am I ever glad to see you, Pat."

For a moment I thought Smythe was going to embrace me. Robert Alexander Smythe is the neighborhood beat cop, one of the few left in the department who prefers walking a beat to riding in a patrol car. He is well known and well liked in this neighborhood and he knows the victim. For this reason, his frustration is even more acute. He feels she should trust him enough to talk to him

Smythe graduated in the same academy class as I. He was what one would describe as a typical "male chauvinist," that is to say I would have described him as such when I first met him. Twenty four weeks and many hours of hard work later, we were fellow officers and friends. We still occasionally have our moments but mostly he just likes to get a "rise" out of me.

Bob was born to the good life with the proverbial silver spoon in his mouth. His father is a third generation New Yorker who inherited his money from a childless uncle who was elected to the U.S. Senate while still in his early thirties. Interested in seeing more Blacks in the political arena, he had high hopes his son would follow in his footsteps and never reconciled to Bob's career choice. His mother, on the other hand, was convinced her son was destined to save the world and would expound on his "mission in life" at every opportunity. This was cause for some disharmony at home as one might imagine.

Bob never married. Between his salary and his independent wealth, he could be described as "sitting pretty." His reluctance to marry may have stemmed from concern that he was being tagged for his money. In fact, he seemed to even avoid casual dating. Instead, he absorbed himself in his job. "His beat," where "his people" needed "his protection," was all the life he seemed to need.

I motioned Bob aside, out of earshot of the victim.

"Give me whatever details you have Bob."

It seems he was only about a block away when he heard the call on his mobile radio and started running. Before he made it halfway down the block, he saw McDoud's unit come screaming across the sidewalk and into the service alley. The car had been coming towards him with the headlights in his face so it wasn't until it turned into the alley that he realized it was a squad car.

McDoud, as it turns out, was just returning to duty from his dinner break and was less than half a block away. In fact, he arrived at the scene so quickly, he could see the two bodies struggling in the alley before the dispatcher had finished her broadcast and had left his unit without stopping to communicate with her. His sergeant will most likely have something to say to him about that later, but for the moment, he is the hero of the hour, especially to the victim. As a matter of fact, Officer McDoud had driven his unit over a part of the sidewalk and into the alley to within six feet of the struggle before exiting his vehicle. His action had prevented the actual rape. The assailant was so intent upon his assault he hadn't noticed the officer or his car.

"I wasn't able to get much from the victim. She says she was waiting for the late bus. She'd just left work at the market two blocks away. She's a clerk there."

"Was that all you could get?"

"That's all."

I walked over to the small figure huddled, completely hidden, under the blanket and sat down on the curb beside her. Gently I tried to fold the blanket away from her face. My efforts were met with resistance and a burst of sobs. I didn't force it. She started rocking backward and forward as if she were in a rocking chair. Without attempting to impede the rocking, I reached out and laid my hand on top of the blanket.

"Ma'am, I'm Officer Salema."

With my free hand, I motioned for Angel and Bob to back away. They understood my signal and retreated. While I concentrated on trying to communicate with the woman, they directed their attention to reducing the size of the audience. Angel then moved our squad unit so that it acted as a screen, giving the victim some measure of privacy. I had hopes I could coax her into the back seat of the squad car for greater privacy but I wasn't going to rush that idea.

I waited for the burst of sobs to subside a bit before making another bid for communication.

"Ma'am," I tried again. "I'm Officer Salema. Will you try to talk to me? I just want to help you."

I think the sound of a female voice finally got through to her, because slowly, very slowly, the blanket parted and I could see a tangled mass of dark hair. The face that turned to me is probably a pretty one but right now no one would describe it as such. A large gash split the brow above her right eye and dried blood marked a trail down to the tip of her chin. Her shoulder-length hair was matted with the overflow. Her lower lip and left jaw were swollen and already turning a peculiar shade of bluish purple. She must have left work in her uniform because I could make out the words

"Handy Mart" above the pocket of her torn smock.

"My purse, where's my purse?"

The words were the first she'd spoken to me. I tried to assure her the purse was safe. Bob Smythe had put it into our squad car but for some reason she insisted on having it. I called out to Bob and Angel.

"Will one of you please bring the lady's purse?"

Bob retrieved the bag and brought it to her. When he handed it to her, she grabbed it to her body in a bear hug as if the familiar item was a life ring thrown to someone drowning. She didn't open it or check the contents; just continued to clutch it tightly with both arms.

I waited for her to relax a bit then slowly, very slowly, I began to extract her story.

She got off work a little later than usual and missed her regular bus by about ten minutes. This time of night the buses run about an hour apart so she knew she'd have to wait. She had been waiting only about ten minutes when a teenage boy walked up and sat on the other end of the bench. He kept staring at her and smiling. Not wanting to be rude, she smiled back.

Suddenly he jumped up, grabbed her purse, heaved it into the alley behind the large apartment building and sat back down with a grin on his face.

She shouted at him saying something like 'What did you do that for?' then ran to retrieve her belongings. The boy followed her as she neared the alley entry; he grabbed her and dragged her all the way in. He started tearing at her clothing but never spoke a word. Before she knew it, they were rolling around on the pavement.

"I was so scared. I thought he was going to kill me. I started screaming and fighting but he was a lot stronger than me. Then suddenly, a big hand reached in and lifted him right off me. I could hear this voice saying over and over, 'you lousy punk, you lousy punk,' then I saw the uniform. There was a police car close by too. I didn't even see it drive up. I guess the guy didn't either, because he was really shocked too."

Her story was slow starting, but once she started talking, it spewed out like water bursting from behind a breached dam. It was as if in telling it quickly and completely she could rid herself of the fright and the bad memories. I could have told her it doesn't work that way, but unfortunately, she will find that out for herself in due time.

As she was nearing the conclusion of her story, I felt rather than saw someone hovering nearby. I refocused my gaze from the victim's face to the building just beyond the squad unit. An elderly woman was standing there with a look of intense concern on her face and her hands clasped below her chin in what could have been an attitude of prayer. I motioned for her to come forward; her response was immediate and eager.

"I'm Mrs. Monahan, Miriam Monahan. I live in this building. When the police arrived I came out to see what happened. I brought that blanket for the young lady. She looked so helpless. It was all I could think to do to help. Is she okay? Is there anything else I can do?"

"That was very thoughtful of you, Ma'am. By any chance did you see any of what happened? I mean here in the alley?"

"No, I live near the front. My apartment only has windows that face the street."

When she noticed the victim starting to remove the blanket, she quickly added,

"No, no, you keep it. If you're ever by, here again you can bring it back but I don't need it right now, and you do. Please keep it as long as you need to."

Then to me, she said,

"Would you like to bring her inside? She may feel more comfortable. You're both more than welcome."

I called out to Bob who rushed right over. Tipping his hat to the elderly woman, he greeted her by name then turned to me with a questioning look.

"We're going to continue this interview inside. Mrs. Monahan has kindly offered the sanctuary of her home. Has Angel been able to reach this young woman's family yet?"

"Great idea. We got a hold of her husband, he's on his way." Then to the elderly woman, he said, "Thank you, Mrs. M., I'll stop in for my usual coffee in the morning."

Mrs. Monahan literally beamed at "Officer Bob" as she shuffled towards the front steps of the apartment building, leading us to her small home. Once inside, she offered us seating in the small sitting room, then headed off to the next room.

"Make yourselves comfortable. I'll make us some tea," said Mrs. M., disappearing.

Mrs. Monahan must have had to pick the tea leaves and go to the well for the water because she made herself invisible for the better part of a half an hour. She was kindly allowing us some time for private discourse while trying not to be too obvious.

Eventually, she emerged from her kitchen with a tray. There were three cups, a teapot and a dish of cookies to go with the tea. I could feel my young victim begin to relax as she was handed a cup of steaming liquid. Mrs. Monahan must be a wizard or a magician.

Sipping my cup of tea, I began to look around. This was a very neat, well kept room. One wall was almost completely covered with what were probably family pictures. Closer observation showed most of the photos were of the same man and a young

woman at various ages. When she noticed me studying the pictures, she volunteered,

"My husband, God rest his soul and our daughter. She would be
about your age now. I lost my husband last year. Reba, our only
child, was killed in a plane crash ten years ago. She was a steward-
ess, you know. Everyone loved her."

Her reminiscing was interrupted by a knock on the door and a
voice called out.

"It's Officer Bob, Mrs. M."

"It's not locked," was her reply.

Bob Smythe entered the room followed closely by a man with
an anxious look on his face. The minute he spotted the blanket
draped figure on the sofa, he rushed to gather her up in his arms.
Almost immediately there was a new rush of sobs as they stood
locked together in the middle of the room. While Bob and I tried
to make ourselves a part of the wallpaper, Mrs. M. quietly slipped
away to the kitchen and returned with two more cups. She filled
the cups, gave one to Bob then like a fussy mother hen she put her
arms around the embracing couple and herded them back to the
sofa.

"Sit, sit, be comfortable. Have a cup of tea. Stay as long as you
need to."

So saying, she pressed a full cup into the man's hands and refilled
the lady's cup as well. The gratitude in both their faces was all the
thanks she required.

"Her husband," Bob said to me from the corner of his mouth.

I just nodded.

Bob and I waited until the couple had time to calm down, then
we related the entire story to the young lady's husband. Maria
and Renaldo Cervantes sat quietly listening. Occasionally Maria

interjected a comment but for the most part she agreed with what I was putting in my report.

We recommended they stop at the local hospital to check on Maria's injuries but now that I had what I needed for my report, they were free to leave.

We said our goodbyes to Mrs. M. and left the apartment. As the door closed behind us I heard that lovely lady saying,

"You two just stay as long as you like but you really should go see a doctor."

I looked at Bob and shook my head.

"Are all the people on your beat like her?"

"Well, not exactly but everyone around here refers to Mrs. M. as 'our neighborhood grandma.' She's all alone, and we all look after her. She makes us coffee and tea and cookies. It's a perfect working arrangement."

"We could use a lot more like her."

Bob just kept nodding his head.

I didn't say anything to him, but I made a mental note to keep this address in mind the next time Angel and I needed a good, hot cup of tea.

"Four Charles six."

"Four Charles six, go ahead." I could tell the dispatcher was in the middle of a yawn.

"Four Charles six, clear and heading for the barn."

Angel is driving now and I am catching up on my notes. It will be at least another hour of report writing in the ready room before I can head home. This last call already has us about two hours into overtime. I can use the extra money but I prefer just getting off on time.

"You'll have company, looks like McDoud is going to rack up some overtime as well."

I gave Angel a dirty look.

"Are you really able to read my mind or have you planted a bug in my brain. Besides I'm going to need a supplementary from you, too."

"I know, but that won't take me too long. All I did was secure the perimeter. You and McDoud did all the work."

The grin on his face was almost more than I could stand. I reached over and smacked him on the back of his head.

"Hey, what was that for?"

"That's for the next time."
I hadn't been able to wipe the grin off his face but I felt better anyway. We pulled the unit into the secure parking lot, gathered up the shotgun and our personal stuff and headed into the building. We always collect our personal things at the end of watch with the hope we'll find a new unit waiting for us at the beginning of the next shift. It hasn't happened yet. Maybe I should get Mrs. M. to cast one of her magic spells.

❖ ❖ ❖

CHAPTER TWO

DAY OFF

The alarm jolted me out of a dead sleep. Someday I'm going to shoot that damned clock. For a moment I couldn't remember why I'd set it. If I'm not mistaken, today is my day off. Then reality set in. I have to be in court. Does it ever end?

I staggered into the bathroom and into the shower. I am not a "morning person," in fact, I have half a mind to talk our legislators into outlawing mornings altogether.

I was washed, dressed and on my way downtown in less than half an hour. Ironically, this was a more or less "cut and dried'" case, yet the defendant insisted on pleading "not guilty."

Angel was waiting for me on the courthouse steps.

"I'll bet that jerk pleaded 'not guilty' just so I wouldn't be able to sleep in on my day off.'"

"My, aren't we testy. Still trying to get them to outlaw morning?"

Chuckling out loud, Angel ducked as my purse whizzed over his head.

"Come on, I'll buy you a cup of tea in the cafeteria. We have at least forty minutes."

Angel bounced up the steps taking them two at a time. Boy, do I hate morning people. There ought to be a law against them, too.

Three cups of tea and dozens of yawns later, we walked into the courtroom. We spent exactly ten minutes in that court: long enough for the judge to seat himself and for the defense attorney to declare,

"Your Honor, my client has decided to change his plea to 'no contest' and throw himself on the mercy of the court."

"I knew it! He just wanted to rob me of my sleep like he robbed that little old lady in the park."

It didn't help a bit that Angel started laughing out loud as soon as the courtroom doors closed behind us.

Angel was still chuckling as we parted company on the sidewalk. For whatever good it did, I grouched and grumbled all the way to my car. That jerk had had the last laugh after all.

I drove straight home. I'd purchased a brand new, super soft sofa just days before and thoughts of stretching out for a nap were all-consuming. I punched the remote door opener, pulled into the garage and shut off the motor. As I started to exit the vehicle, I could swear I heard a noise. I sat very still for a moment and strained my ears. Nothing but silence.

"Guess I'm starting to hear things in my old age,' I spoke out loud.

I gathered up my purse, climbed out of the car, hung the car keys on a peg near the door jamb, pushed the button on the garage door controls and opened the door leading from the garage into the kitchen. I do not know what prompted it but as I stepped across the threshold the hair at the nape of my neck bristled and goosebumps ran the length of my frame. Every sense was suddenly on alert and I froze. Very slowly I reached behind to my waistband and removed the Smith & Wesson five-shot I carry off duty.

Then I heard that noise again, only this time it was louder. I quietly lowered my purse to the floor and with my heart pounding in my throat I slowly crept across the kitchen. The noise had come from somewhere in the back of the house.

I peeked around through the open door and now I could hear more noises as if someone was ransacking through cupboards and drawers. I peered over the dining table towards the front door. Somehow I was not surprised to see several items of mine neatly stacked as if waiting for some donation collection.

I didn't know how many intruders I was about to face but at least all the noise seemed to be coming from the same direction: the master bedroom. While I was deciding on my next move, the decision was made for me. Casually strolling down the hall towards me with his arms laden with a suitcase and three large, very full plastic bags, was a tall, thin man in a hooded sweatshirt.

We saw each other at about the same time. Before I could find my voice he dropped what he was carrying and made a flying dive right through the glass of the nearest window. I rushed to the front door and charged outside just in time to see the man running off down the street.

Frantically digging for my cell phone, I started running after him. I dialed 911 and requested back up without breaking stride. I have made a point of keeping up on my physical health, so even though he had a bit of a head start on me, I had no trouble catching up to him. My burglar friend was obviously not too familiar with the neighborhood, because he took a couple of wrong turns and found himself cornered against a high fence.

Pointing my weapon directly at the middle of his chest, I ordered him to the ground and he nervously complied.

"Hey lady, don't shoot, okay. Be careful with that thing, okay."

Per Department regulations, I identified myself as a peace officer then ordered him to roll over on his stomach and place his hands behind his head.

With an incredulous expression, he shouted, "You're a cop?"

"You're damned right I am! Do as I told you now, get down, roll over and put your hands behind your head."

Backing away from me in a seated position, he suddenly flipped over onto all fours, stood up and raising his middle finger over his head in the universally recognized "salute," he yelled, "f--- you lady," climbed over that fence and started running again.

As long as this guy thought I was just some crazy dame with a gun, he complied with all my instructions. When he found out I was an officer, he knew I couldn't shoot. He obviously knew the law, as well as I. Identifying myself worked against me but I had no choice. I started after him but by the time I recovered from my surprise and scaled that fence, he really had the advantage and I lost him.

I heard sirens as my back-up came screaming around the comer. We searched the area for a while but came up empty-handed.

The squad unit gave me a lift home and as I exited the vehicle, I noticed there was a strange car parked just down the street from my house.

The two officers and I exchanged "What the heck, why not" looks, and they ran the plates. The registration came back to a recently released parolee who had done time for: what else? House burglary.

"I'm off duty, guys, you handle it, okay?"

"Sure, Pat, but we'll need a 'supp' from you for the report."

"I'll do it in the morning. Right now, I need my beauty sleep."

Mumbling to myself about getting a house alarm or a dog, I entered my home and started putting my things back where they belonged. Gratefully nothing was broken but the window; guess he wanted to be sure he got his money's worth at the pawnshop. Once everything was shipshape again, I made a stiff cup of tea, turned on the TV, and cuddled into that new sofa. Guess the good Lord agreed I deserved a rest because even the phone was silent for the rest of the evening.

I rolled over in bed the following morning and again threatened to shoot my alarm clock. Today was also supposed to be my day off, but I have to go to the office and write that supplemental burglary report.

I dragged myself out of bed, did what I could in the bathroom to make myself look half human, dressed and headed for the car. Since both my days off are about shot anyway, I might as well use what's left to shop for a home security system. I had planned to get one; this incident just gave me the boost I needed.

Down at the office, I made my way to the report writing room intending to dash off a quick "supp" and be on my way. Well, fate had other plans for me.

"Hey, Pat," called the duty desk sergeant, "they want you up in the Dick's Division."

"What for?" I yelled back

"Something about a line up over last night's arrest."

"Line up? Are you kidding?"

Grumbling out loud, I headed out the door and down the hall to the elevator. The Detective Division is on the fifth floor. After all that running last night, there is no way I'm taking the stairs.

As I walked through the door of the Burglary Detail, I could see the two officers from last night's incident in deep conversation with a plain clothes detective. When they saw me they both started talking at once.

"Whoa, guys, slow down, one at a time."

I finally managed to piece the story together. It seems our parolee was the owner of that car, alright, but he wasn't the one driving it. He loaned it to his "friend" who used it to commit the burglary, then ran off and left it behind. When the officers showed up at the parolee's house to place him under arrest, his "old lady" wasn't about to let him take the fall for someone else. She fingered the "friend," and now I have to pick him out of a line-up.

"This is supposed to be my day off, you guys. I feel like giving that jerk a knuckle sandwich."

The frosting on the cake was when the desk sergeant called out to me as I was leaving the building,

"Hey, Pat, how come you don't have a house alarm?"

"Just lucky, I guess," I called over my shoulder as I breezed out the door.

"Smart Alec," I mumbled under my breath.

◆ ◆ ◆

CHAPTER THREE

SHIFT FROM HELL

It has been the "Shift from Hell." There were back to back calls all night and nothing simple. We will be hours overtime at the end of shift; there have been only brief periods of downtime during the night when we could catch up on reports. We have forty minutes before we can "head for the barn" and start writing.

We had worked right through dinner break and I am starving. We pulled into a drive-through fast food joint. Our unit was positioned with a clear view of the intersection and we were waiting for our order. The light was red, and there was only one vehicle, a small blue compact, waiting for it to turn. Suddenly we could hear a racing engine; something was approaching and it was going fast.

"Sounds like some one's in a hurry."

The words were hardly out of Angel's mouth when a speeding sedan came up over the railroad tracks and struck that small compact from behind. It hit the other car with such tremendous force it drove it across the intersection and head-on into a telephone pole. Angel hit the lights and siren and the patrol unit leaped out of the drive up lane and into the street. I was already calling for back up and ambulance. There's no way someone isn't hurt in that mess.

We were on the site in seconds. There had been this eerie silence immediately following the grinding sound of the crash. Now steam was rising from both vehicles. Fortunately there was no fire. Angel positioned the squad car behind the sedan, which was in the middle of the intersection, so the flashing lights could serve as a warning to other drivers. Next, he attended to the driver of that vehicle. I ran across to the compact.

That little compact was totaled. Amazingly the headlights were still burning though now they were wrapped around the pole and facing one another. Inside the vehicle was a young couple. Their guardian angels must have been riding with them because, except for a few cuts and bruises, they were not seriously hurt. The initial impact had severed the bolts at the bottom of the front seat, throwing it backward. When their vehicle hit that pole, they were flat on their backs and the majority of the force was absorbed by the bottom of the upholstered car seat.

The driver of the sedan was hurt more seriously but nothing life threatening. He was a male, approximately fifty years old and so drunk he thought I was a taxi driver and kept trying to hire me to drive him home. His vehicle was also totaled. It seems he'd just left the bar on the other side of the railroad tracks and was heading home (he said). According to his driver's license, "home" was actually in the opposite direction. Because of his injuries, he went to the hospital in an ambulance but under arrest. In spite of the fact he was now communicating with us, we believe he had passed out at the wheel and was unconscious when he hit that other car.

We were able to reach the parents of the young lady in the compact and they responded to the scene. They refused the ambulance ride for their daughter but promised they would seek medical advice before going home.

It was another two hours before we were cleared to leave that scene. Even though the tow trucks had removed both vehicles, we had to finish our investigation. We may have to testify on this one so we want to make sure all our I's are dotted and our T's are crossed. When we left, the traffic guys were still doing their thing and the intersection was still partially closed. Angel and I never did get our meals and it was almost daylight when I finally got home. My bed never looked so good.

◆ ◆ ◆

CHAPTER FOUR

LOVING PICNICS

I'm riding alone tonight; Angel called in sick. It's Wednesday, and there's not a whole lot happening out in the real world. I had only two bookings and they were nothing critical.

I helped an out of town couple find their way back to the Inter-State, made a welfare check on Mrs. M (she sure makes a great cup of tea), called Angel during my dinner break and right now, I am cruising around, marking time until the end of shift.

"Four Charles six."

The sound of the radio nearly startled me out of my socks. It had been silent most of the shift.

"Four Charles six, go ahead."

"Four Charles eight requests back up; seventeen hundred block of Johnson Avenue; injured child; ambulance is en route; code three."

"Four Charles six, check."

My heart began to pound like a hammer against my breastbone. Adrenalin raced through my veins like an electric shock. The unit roared into life as I activated the lights and siren and pulled out into the traffic lane. Code three is always a rush but when a child is involved, it's different.

Johnson Avenue is in the beat that abuts mine and is only about a quarter mile from the confluence of the two areas. I drove as fast as I could while keeping department policy and safety in mind.

As I approached Johnson Avenue, I didn't have to wonder where it was I was needed. Four Charles eight was parked at the curb and his lights were still activated. I pulled up behind the other unit and bailed out of the car at a dead run. The front door of the house was open and a young boy with panic written across his tear-streaked face was motioning me from the porch.

I took the steps of the porch two at a time and burst through the open door. Officer Mike McDoud was on his knees bent over the form of a naked little girl, probably not more than two years old. His mouth was pressed firmly to the child's, and in between breaths he was growling,

"Breath, damn it, breath."

Throwing my clipboard and keys to the floor, I dove in beside him.

"Take a rest, I've got it."

Sliding my hand under the shoulders of the limp form, I took over from McDoud.
The cadence started in my mind almost automatically,

"Three breaths, two chest depressions, three breaths, two chest depressions."

Taking turns, McDoud and I continued CPR until the ambulance arrived and the EMTs took over.

By the time they performed their miracles and drove off to the hospital, the little girl had begun to respond but just barely. She wasn't out of the woods yet and there is always the issue of brain damage.

Standing on the sidewalk, I watched the ambulance round the

corner and head towards downtown and the nearest hospital, Mission General. McDoud tossed me a quick salute and climbed into his patrol unit. He'll be following the ambulance to ER to get a statement from the child's parents. It has fallen to me to interview any witnesses at the scene and wrap things up here.

From what little we were able to piece together here at the scene, it seems the little girl was in the bathtub, the father was watching TV and the mother got a phone call. When she finished her phone conversation and returned to the bathroom, she found the child face down in the water.

I finished my interviews and headed into the office. McDoud was not there and still hadn't returned by the time I finished my reports. I had a tough time getting the picture of that little girl's face out of my mind. I changed out of my uniform and walked out to my car. I pulled out of the parking lot and hesitated only a few seconds before turning left towards the hospital. Maybe McDoud will need help with his interviews.

When I walked into the Emergency waiting room I could see McDoud sitting in a chair at a small table in the far corner. As I neared the table I noticed there was no paperwork in sight.

"You still working on those reports?"

"Well, no. I got what I need and it's all here in my briefcase. What are you doing here?"

"Oh, I thought you might need some help with your reports and I had no plans tonight, anyway. How's the kid?"

"Not too good."

"Will they let us see her?"

"Yeah, I've been in there a couple times myself."

I walked over to the nurses' desk, identified myself and asked if it was okay for me to see the child. She asked me to wait and walked away from the desk. In a few minutes she returned and said,

"Just follow me, officer."

When I walked into the room in ICU, for a moment I thought the bed was empty. That little body hardly made a bump in the bedding. The woman seated beside the bed turned and when she saw me, she came rushing over with tears streaming down her face. Throwing both her arms around my neck, she silently clung to me. We stood there embracing for several seconds then she pulled away and gazed into my face. Gratitude was shining from her eyes though she didn't speak a single word. She didn't have to.

I went over to the bed and stared down at the tiny being now fighting for her life. The face was ashen, there were tubes connecting her to machines and monitors but she was breathing. My heart ached for these two parents who are sitting here praying for the life of their child and no doubt blaming themselves for nearly losing her.

I returned to the waiting room and sat down with McDoud.

"How long are you going to stay here, Mike?

"I'll be heading for the barn in just a few," he replied. "I have to file these reports before I leave tonight. I hope that kid makes it."

We walked out to the parking lot together. I climbed into my old sedan and sat there totally exhausted. Every muscle in my body ached. I hated the thought of going home to my empty house. I dialed Angel and asked how he'd like to buy an old friend a cup of tea.

"I'll put the kettle on the burner but remember I've got some sort of bug and I don't know if I'm contagious."

"I just need to talk."

"You got it," was all he said.

When I entered Angel's house, it was obvious he had been busy performing some more of his special magic. There was a warm fire on the hearth, a tray sat nearby with two cups and a full teapot, the sofa had been made up with bedding, and a pair of polka dot pajamas was draped over the arm.

"Angel's Homespun Hotel and psychiatric couch at your service."

"Someone ought to take out a patent on you," I chuckled.

"Here's an extra toothbrush. Grab the P.J.s and go clean up. I'll have your tea ready when you get back. I'm not letting you go home in this frame of mind but I'm the sickie so I get the bed and you get the couch."

I didn't even try to argue. By the time I got back to the living room my tea was waiting and Angel was kicked back in his recliner with a steaming cup in his hands.

"Okay, talk."

And talk I did. I started with tonight's incident with the child and before I realized it, I was telling him about my carefully kept secret: that I had been a victim of an assault and near rape years ago. I talked, and he listened until almost dawn. Three pots of tea and several fire logs later, I found I could hardly keep my eyes open.

"Well, Dr. Angel, I think I am talked out and about to fall asleep. Thank you, my friend. You've bailed me out again."

"Sleep tight, see you in the morning," he said as he collected the cups and headed for the kitchen. I nestled into that cozy sofa and pulled the covers up over my shoulders. I don't remember seeing him leave the kitchen.

Three weeks almost to the day since McDoud and I labored over that little girl, I reported to work and found a note in my mail slot. It was an invitation to a picnic and it was from the parents of that child. Attached to the invitation was a note from my sergeant saying McDoud and I were being given time off during the shift to attend the function.

Mike and I pulled up to the park and could see a very active, very healthy little girl in a bright-pink dress running around chasing a run away balloon. I felt a lump develop in my throat. We had touched base with these folks and knew the girl had recovered but somehow it was different seeing her look so normal. Mike and I gave each other a big "high five" and went over to see what was smelling so good. I love picnics!

◆ ◆ ◆

CHAPTER FIVE

SWIVEL HOLSTER
FOR SALE

I used to enjoy being a training officer. It was a challenge that's true, but the end results were often rewarding. That was before I got so lazy. Not only is it a big responsibility but there's all that extra paperwork at the end of the shift. Now, when my day is over I just want to go home and relax.

I must have been feeling particularly soft in the head that day because when the sergeant asked me to take on a trainee, I said, "Okay." This recruit isn't all that new, he's on the last stage of the four weeks OJT (on job training) phase of instruction but most of the other FTOs (field training officers) were occupied so rather than make him wait, I took on the job.

I could tell from the night we were introduced, this guy was a little different. I described him as a "my way" guy. He's one who will have to learn the hard way that "his way" will not always work.

Kevin Watson was a surprise. He topped the chart at approximately six feet seven inches and weighed in at just under two hundred and sixty-five pounds: not exactly what I'd call a little guy. Our Department had a minimum height limit and a maximum height limit at that time of 5' 9" to 6' 6". Watson exceeded the maximum. When I asked him about it, he stated, "Definitely I'll deny I said it if you snitch, but I scrunched down a bit when they measured me."

"Hey, as long as you can do the job, it's no skin off my nose. I don't agree with those damned limits anyway."

Our chief did not like swivel holsters but though he strongly discouraged their use, he never actually outlawed them. Kevin liked swivel holsters and chose to ignore his boss's conviction.

Those squad units were not built with someone Kevin's size in mind. They were cramped even for the "average Joe." Watching him literally fold himself into the passenger seat every night was nothing short of hilarious. I think he had the longest legs in the entire world.

Our shift usually ended at midnight. Around eleven-thirty the dispatcher's voice broke the silence:

"Four Charles six."

"Four Charles six, go ahead."

Even the mic looked too small in Kevin's hands.

"Burglary in progress Fourteen Sixteen Coldwater Avenue. Neighbor says occupants are on vacation. Code three. What's your ETA?"

"Four Charles six, check. ETA about four."

Activating the lights and siren, I made a left at the next block and headed uphill towards The Heights, a rather upscale section of town.

Several blocks from our destination, I killed the siren and then a few blocks farther along, I doused the lights as well. Just before turning onto Coldwater, I shut off the headlights. We knew the address we were looking for was about midway on the block, so I killed the engine and we silently slid to the curb two houses short of that destination.

We unhooked our lap belts and started to exit the unit. That is when our world fell apart.

Kevin swung those long legs out of the unit and in one fluid motion followed with the rest of his body. Well the seat belt got tangled in his swivel holster and before he could help himself, he was pitched face and belly down onto the pavement.

Seeing him start to fall, I made a flying dive to try and grab him. Well in those old squad cars, the emergency equipment was located on the steering wheel. As I reached out for him, my arm flipped the light switch to the "on" position. Realizing what I'd done I abandoned my efforts at saving Kevin and dove back to shut off the lights. Groping for the switch, I accidentally activated the siren. It all happened in seconds.

So here we were, two houses from our "burglary in progress" with lights and siren going full blast and one of the responding officers face down in the street trying to extricate himself from a seat belt.

As quickly as possible I shut down the lights but we had to listen to that old centrifugal siren slowly wind itself down. It seemed to take forever. Kevin finally got free of the seat belt, picked himself off the pavement, dusted off the front of his uniform and attempted to regain some semblance of his dignity.

I sheepishly crawled out of the driver's seat and as I did so, the light on the porch just in front of our squad unit flicked on. Standing on the porch in his bathrobe, hands on his hips and shaking his head was a witness to our display of "Police efficiency": the citizen who had called in the initial burglary report. Still shaking his head, he silently turned and went back into his house.

The longest road I've had to travel in a very long time was from that squad unit to the front door of that man's house, for as difficult as it was going to be, we had to go up and make contact with him. Needless to say, our burglar was probably long gone but we had to conclude our investigation and file a report. That required us to interview the complainant.

We didn't bother trying to explain our predicament to that fine citizen; anything we said would only have served to make things worse. He was going to think what he was going to think. Hopefully, if we have any further contact with him in the future, our actions then may serve to exonerate us.

We touched base with John Q. Citizen then went over to check on the victim's residence. If it could be said there was anything positive about the situation, it would have to be that our spectacular arrival appeared to have scared away the burglar before he succeeded in entering the premises. Evidence of his attempts were, however, clearly visible but as we were to learn later from the homeowner, nothing was missing outside either.

We re-contacted the complainant, concluded our interview, then crept back to the unit with our tails between our legs. We reported "call cleared" to the dispatcher and headed for the garage: a pair of not very happy campers.

Then we had to pray our fellow officers never found out about our little fiasco. God help us if they ever did.

Kevin wasn't off the hook entirely, however. I suggested he should consider patenting his unusual method of burglary response as a sort of Crime Prevention Program. His "drop-dead" look told me he did not entirely appreciate my brand of humor.

The following evening, when Kevin reported for duty, there was no sign of the offending swivel holster and later that week, I noticed a sign on the bulletin board in the Ready Room:

FOR SALE, SLIGHTLY USED SWIVEL HOLSTER. MAKE BEST OFFER.

Case closed, we hoped.

Oh, yes, Kevin did successfully complete his OJT training phase and went on to become a competent officer.

◆ ◆ ◆

CHAPTER SIX

IGNORING
PROCEDURES

I t had been a while since I'd made a booking at the County Jail. Our department had temporary holding cells at each of the substations. That was not just as a convenience for the patrol officers but to keep them in their beats. The alternative was for officers to make the long trip out to the County Jail to book a prisoner leaving their beats unstaffed for extended periods.

Early in my career, I had a close friend who was a Deputy Sheriff. At that time, Jan Wyatt worked nights (swing shift) at the jail and when we got together socially we often swapped "war stories."

She had been working that particular shift for about a year. At the time there was only one female officer assigned to the women's section during the night shift. This made things rather harrowing for that officer because whenever someone booked a female prisoner, the officer had to lock down her section and go to the Booking Office to receive and collect that prisoner, basically leaving the housing unit unattended.

One particular night had been unusually busy. Jan had been in and out of the women's section so often there may as well have been a revolving door.

Early in the shift she booked a young alcoholic who was carried in, kicking and screaming. This young woman, we'll call her Mary was a regular who was well known to the beat officers and the jail staff. She always came in violent but usually became almost docile once she sobered up. She was deaf, mute and communicated mostly through sign language.

Upon her arrival, Mary was placed into one of the security cells for her own protection. These cells had no beds just a mattress on the floor and were equipped with flushable toilets that were basically just holes in the floor with a flush button.

Not exactly **The Ritz.** Jan told it like this:

Towards the end of the shift, when I returned from yet another booking, Mary began pleading to be transferred to a standard cell. She appeared to have sobered quite a bit and managed to convince me she would cooperate.

Now there was a safety procedure on the night shift: no prisoners could be relocated unless two officers were present. I knew this and should have followed regulations BUT I also knew everyone was exceptionally busy and I made the mistake of believing I knew this woman well enough to trust moving her without waiting for back up.

The operating system which controlled the cell doors made it possible to open specific doors or all of the doors by simply selecting the number and turning a wheel. These controls were located behind a locked panel and situated at the front of the corridor which led to the bank of cells. I informed Mary I would open two doors: the one on the cell she was occupying and the one on the cell to which she was being moved.

Since I was not completely fluent in sign language, I wrote her a note which said,

'When I open the doors, I want you to leave the security cell, walk down the hall and enter the only other door you will find open. Do you understand and agree?'

Mary nodded vigorously but when I opened those doors, that woman exited the security cell, looked over her shoulder at me, then ran like a rabbit all the way to the far end of the corridor and climbed the bars up to the ceiling.

I closed and locked the security control panel and went after her. I threatened, I begged, I pleaded, I climbed after her and tried to drag her down by the legs. Nothing worked.

I was left with no alternative but to call down to Main Control and ask for help. That was one of the most difficult calls I ever had to make. The lieutenant on duty happened to be one who already disliked female officers and me in particular. Naturally, he felt it necessary to personally accompany the two officers who responded to my request for assistance. And naturally, I not only got a royal butt chewing, but I also got a letter of reprimand in my personnel file.

Mary paid a price, too. She had to stay in that security cell until her court hearing two days later.

I learned two valuable lessons. Rules and regulations are created for a purpose and it's probably not smart to risk ticking off your boss especially when he already doesn't like you.

◆ ◆ ◆

CHAPTER SEVEN

LOST NEAR
LINDA ROAD

It hadn't been particularly busy during the shift, just enough to keep time from dragging. I was riding alone again and I'd cleared my last call about ten minutes earlier. I was about to take my meal break when the radio came alive.

"Four Charles six."

"Four Charles six, go ahead."

"Report to Sgt. Kendrick, beat eight, Linda Road and Fifth. Assist in perimeter search."

"Four Charles six check. Code?"

"Four Charles six, code two."

"Four Charles six, check."

I have never liked rolling "code two" which means "get there as fast as you can with caution but no lights or siren." Some departments have actually discontinued its use. I wish ours would follow suit.

I headed for the vicinity of beat eight. It is around three in the morning, so traffic is light. Linda Road is a pretty well known street but I have never worked that beat, and I am unfamiliar with most of the cross streets and landmarks.

I found Sgt. Kendrick without much difficulty and he told me we were saturating the area looking for a home invasion suspect. The incident occurred less than fifteen minutes earlier. A male, no description had broken into the home of an elderly woman beat her pretty severely and stolen her purse.

I started driving up and down the side streets, keeping an eye peeled for anything unusual. It was pretty frustrating because we had no suspect description. The streets were empty and I had been driving for at least twenty minutes with no luck when suddenly, some movement caught my attention in an alley behind a large building. I was approaching a large intersection at the time. I backed the unit up, switched off the lights, and nosed into the entrance of the alley. Seated on a curb behind the building was a man who appeared to be rifling through something at his feet. I exited my vehicle, drew my weapon, then reached inside and turned the headlights back on.

Staying behind the vehicle door, I called out to him.

"This is the police, stay where you are and put your hands in the air where I can see them."

The man looked towards me but instead of complying with my directions, he grabbed the item at his feet, jumped up and started running away from me. Coming from behind the door, I gave chase. As it turned out, the alley was a blind one and he soon found himself facing a very tall fence with nowhere else to go. He attempted to scale the fence and may have succeeded except for the fact he was reluctant to let go of the item he was carrying: a woman's large purse.

I holstered my weapon, grabbed hold of his pants legs and dragged him to the ground. I threw him to the pavement, drew my weapon again and ordered him to lie on his face with his hands behind his head. Placing one knee into the small of his back and the barrel of my weapon at the base of his skull I warned him to be still.

With my free hand I began calling to the other officers on my remote radio,

"I have suspect in custody, need back up. I am located behind a large tan building."

The Sgt.'s voice squawked in my ear,

"What's your location, Salema?"

"I don't know what street. I am behind a very large tan building, in an alley, near a large intersection."

I could hear other squad cars racing along the streets around me with sirens blaring. Reflections from their emergency lights danced patterns in the nearby trees but no one turned into the alley. I could tell they were searching frantically but it was in vain.

Two or three times more I repeated what I knew of my location but they seemed no closer to finding me.

Finally, I think my prisoner was becoming nervous about being stretched out on the ground with the barrel of a gun pressed to his head, not knowing how edgy I might be or how long this might drag on because, he suddenly volunteered.

"We're behind Payless Drugs."

It startled me and I answered.

"What?"

Shouting now, he repeated,

"We're behind Payless Drugs."

Chuckling, I responded,

"Oh, thanks."

Then in a matter of fact tone, I repeated that direction to my fellow officers.

In seconds, three squad cars wheeled into the alley behind my car and there were blue uniforms all over the place.

Sgt. Kendrick was the last to show.

"Good work, Salema, good work."

In as nonchalant a tone as I could muster, considering my heart rate was probably still about 98, I said,

"Thanks, Sarge."

I returned to my squad car, placed my prisoner in the back seat, then sneaked a hankie from my pocket and mopped the sweat from my forehead. That night after my shift was over, I dug out my City Map and did a little remedial study.

◆ ◆ ◆

CHAPTER EIGHT

WRESTLING MATCH

Angel and I were cruising the beat, just keeping a watchful eye when some activity in front of the Liquor Barn caught my attention.

"Hey Angel, that guy on the corner looks a lot like the sketch they showed us at briefing. You know, the guy that's been hanging around schools trying to pick up young girls."

"Hmm, maybe so. Won't hurt to stop and talk to him, just to touch base and see what's going down."

"What about those other two, the ones he's talking to? Ever seen them around the neighborhood before."

"Nah, they don't look familiar to me. Do they to you?"

"Well, I'm not sure."

"Four Charles six.

"Four Charles six, go ahead," answered the dispatcher.

"We'll be out of the car."

"Four Charles six, check."

Angel pulled the unit up to the curb just a few feet behind where the three men stood talking. I exited the car first and called to the men. Before I could say anything further, one of them broke away from the group and started running. I gave chase. He ran the length of the block then cut across an adjacent field.

I shouted to him several times to stop but to no avail. His path eventually took him into a residential area and he continued his flight across numerous back yards and over fences. I wasn't far behind but I was running short of breath and apparently so was he. I had no trouble keeping up with him but I couldn't seem to overtake him. He climbed one more fence, crossed a small creek then came to a complete stop just short of a local baseball field. It was pretty evident he had run out of gas. I was grateful because my tank was running on empty as well.

Catching up with him, I reached to my holster to draw my weapon and was horrified to find it empty. Before I could rationalize the stupidity of the act, I pointed my empty hand at him with my forefinger extended and shouted,

"Put your hands in the air."

To my amazement, he complied. Convinced he would notice any minute that my hand held no weapon, I panicked and ran up to him and punched him in the face with all my might.

Well, the blow only served to infuriate him and he swung back at me. I ducked but the fight was on. The two of us rolled around on the ground for the better part of five minutes. I kept trying to gain the upper hand but we were both so worn out, I was lucky to hold my own.

In what seemed like hours, I finally heard Angel's voice,

"Hold it right there. Put your hands behind your head."

He had seen the direction in which we were headed and driven the unit around to an area he expected would intercept the fleeing suspect. Thankfully, he guessed right. He hadn't expected me to catch up with the suspect because the man had such a head start. I wish he had been right about that, as well.

At the sound of my partner's voice, the man stopped fighting and got to his knees. He was unable to comply with Angel's order to put his hands anywhere because he was using them to hold himself up.

We were both gasping for air. In between labored breaths I tried to explain to Angel about my missing gun. All he heard was the word "gun" and thought I was saying the man had a gun. He pointed his weapon at the suspect and started shouting at him to drop the gun. The man started waving his hands in the air while I tried desperately to catch my breath. I was afraid Angel would shoot before I could explain. I managed to put a stop to any further violence by waving my hands and shouting,

"Stop. Stop."

My suspect flopped over on his belly with his hands extended outward and just laid there waiting.

Finally, I regained enough of my wind to tell Angel I had lost my weapon somewhere along the trail. Imagine my surprise when he asked,

"Where's your flashlight?"

I slapped my hands to the spot on the Sam Brown belt where the light should have been. It was empty, too. I immediately began to take inventory. I was also missing my radio and my key holder.

We lifted our suspect to a standing position to place him in cuffs and realized he was missing both of his shoes and one of his socks.

"That was one Helluva pursuit!" exclaimed Angel.

Ignoring his comment, I snapped, "You drive back around. I'll retrace my steps and try to find my stuff."

Angel had called for backup before following me. That unit pulled up a few minutes after he had and was now willing to transport our prisoner. I grudgingly accepted Angel's offer to help me in my recovery search.

Taking a good look at my prisoner I realized he was not even the man that had initially drawn our interest.

"Why the Hell did you run?" I yelled at him.

"Well, I saw the cop car stop; I'm on probation and I don't like cops. So, I ran."

I could have slapped him.

Leaving the locked unit, Angel followed me as we retraced my suspect's flight path. We found my weapon in one back yard, my flashlight in another and my key holder with keys dangling from a chain link fence. The suspect's sock was also hanging on that fence. We found his shoes and my radio scattered across the field.

Angel and I did a lot of reflecting on that incident. We finally came to the conclusion I may not have had to fight the man if l hadn't punched him. We decided he was so pooped after that long run, he must not have noticed I had no weapon in my hand when I pointed at him and ordered him to put his hands into the air. Had I not panicked but simply ordered him to turn his back, I could probably have cuffed him and he would not have known the difference until it was too late. We'll never really know but it was sure fun to tell this story. It wasn't so much fun living it.

Most of our colleagues don't believe that really happened so I was spared the usual jokes and harassment.

"Boy, you sure can tell a good story, Salema, you ought to write a book."

I have heard that from more than one listener. Maybe I will.

❖ ❖ ❖

CHAPTER NINE

SALMON STEAK TO GO

"If something can go wrong, it will go wrong." That is a direct quote from Murphy's Law. There isn't an officer I know who is not a firm believer.

I notified the dispatcher I would be out of the unit for my dinner break, seated myself at my favorite far rear table in the only 24-hour restaurant in the beat, ordered my meal and began reviewing my notes from the last call. I was the only customer in the place so it was relatively quiet. It was a later than usual meal break; the shift had really been busy and I was starved. In about ten minutes, the waitress set my plate in front of me. That salmon steak looked and smelled awesome. I was just reaching for my fork when the dispatcher's voice broke the silence.

"Four Charles six."

"Four Charles six, go ahead."

"Fight at Sixteenth and Sheridan, outside Gilroy's Bar. Code three."

Gazing longingly at my steaming plate, I hoisted myself out of the booth and headed for the door.

"Hang onto that for me," I called over my shoulder to the waitress, "I'll be back."

I flipped on the emergency lights, activated the siren and pulled out of the parking lot. I knew there would be other officers dispatched to the scene but Sheridan Avenue was only eight blocks away, so I would likely be the first to arrive.

As I guided the unit through traffic, I could hear my stomach roaring its displeasure at being denied satisfaction.

"Shut up," I growled aloud. "Your time will come."

I turned onto Sheridan a few minutes later and doused the lights and siren. I could see a crowd gathered out in the street. I notified Dispatch of my arrival and was told two other units were just blocks away.

As I exited the unit, I saw two males slugging it out within the circle of onlookers. Fists flying, they seemed intent on pounding the holy begeebers out of each other. No one present seemed to have noticed the squad car pull up. There was no evidence of weapons so I walked slowly hoping one of the other units would arrive before I reached the struggling duo.

Then a woman broke away from the crowd and pounced onto the back of one of the fighters. He immediately whirled and swatted her like a pesky fly, sending her flying across the sidewalk and into a light pole. I had no choice now but to hurry my pace.

Calling to the crowd to back away, I stepped up to the two combatants, drew my baton, and drove it between the two men.

"Okay, you two, knock it off, get back, break it up, this is the police."

Suddenly, two women pounced on my back and the two fighters turned on me as well. I found myself in a swirling mass of arms, legs and fists. I finally managed to extricate myself, back away, and draw my weapon.

"Alright, you guys drop on your bellies," I shouted between gasps for breath.

All four immediately complied and the rest of the crowd backed farther away. My back-up pulled up just then and two officers came running to my defense.

"I got it handled," I gasped. "Just lend me your cuffs."

"Okay, you yoyos, sit up."

Still holding my pistol in my right hand, I tossed the cuffs at them one at a time.

"You hook yourselves together and make it quick."

In no time at all, I had four prisoners cuffed together in a line. My back-up just stood and watched as I had directed them to.

"All right, march!" I yelled, and the line of prisoners headed for my patrol unit.

"Want us to take a couple?" asked one of the other officers.

"Nope, I'm going to teach these drunks a lesson. Look what they did to my uniform and my dinner is sitting on a table back there at Tiny's and is probably ruined and I'm still hungry as a bear."

Then to my "conga line," I ordered,

"Okay, all of you climb into the back seat of my squad car. NOW!"

It was no easy task considering they were all hooked together with cuffs but grumbling and grunting they managed to stuff themselves into that cramped space. The result resembled the proverbial "sardines in a can."

"Meet me down at Booking and you can get your cuffs back," I tossed at the other two officers.

I holstered my weapon and climbed behind the wheel. As I drove away with my pile of humanity in the back seat of the unit, I could see the other two officers standing on the sidewalk laughing and shaking their heads in wonder.

"All right everybody, the show's over, move along, clear the area."

Then the two back-up officers climbed into their units still shaking their heads and headed for the Booking Office.

"That Salema, she's something else."

I never did get back to my salmon steak.

❖ ❖ ❖

CHAPTER TEN

GET ALONG
LITTLE BUCKY

I t isn't often that I reach the end of my shift, look back on my day and not recall at least one incident I would consider really "unusual." The world is a funny place and nothing can be as rewarding or as disappointing as dealing with the public. Gratefully, the scale usually tips to the rewarding side. Sometimes, however, things happen that cannot be placed into either category.

I was sitting in my patrol unit eating my lunch and watching some young boys play basketball in the park. It is one of those small, neighborhood parks with lots of trees, a playground with swings and slides and a concrete pad in one corner just big enough for a single-pole and basket.

As I was washing down the last bite with a rather stale soda, Four Charles eight pulled up beside me. I crawled out of the unit and leaned against one of the front fenders. The other officer did the same. This way we can both get a little air and stretch our limbs but still hear the radios.

Mike McDoud and I had been chatting for about ten minutes when both of our radios sounded off at the same time.

There is a report of a car swerving all over one of the major connector roads, at twenty miles an hour or less. Dispatch is sending both units to intercept, code three.

We are about ten miles from where we stand the best chance of intercepting the driver. Hopefully, he won't cause an accident before we can reach him.

It doesn't take too long before we spot our culprit and give chase. As reported, the small sedan, with one male occupant is traveling approximately twenty miles per hour and weaving all over the road. Other vehicles are swerving around him. Drivers are sitting on their horns and shaking their fists. Fortunately, I am not able to read lips. I pulled in behind the vehicle and McDoud began a zig-zag maneuver behind me to slow the faster-moving traffic.

Neither the siren nor the lights seemed to faze this driver. It must have looked strange from the air: a car and two patrol units weaving their way down the highway. We could almost have been waltzing.

We called for back-up. We're going to try and trap the other vehicle between patrol cars and hopefully bring the driver to a stop on the shoulder of the road.

Suddenly, the driver changed direction and entered an on-ramp onto the freeway. The situation is much more serious now.

"Four Charles six."

"Four Charles six, go ahead."

"This Looney just darted onto the freeway. Where's our back up?"

I wasn't quite able to keep the irritated tone from my voice.

Dispatch informed us two Highway Patrol units were en route and less than two minutes away.

With the help of the additional units, we are finally able to force the driver to the shoulder of the freeway. By now there are two news helicopters circling overhead.

That is when "you-know-what" hit the fan. Before any of the officers are able to exit their units, our suspect comes barreling out
of his vehicle wearing a cowboy hat, cowboy boots, and nothing
else. He races to the center divider of the freeway and starts running and yelling repeatedly,

"Whoopee, get along there, Bucky."

He has a riding crop in his hand and is smacking himself on the
buttocks as he runs. McDoud and I give chase. That dude was fast
and we are burdened with our Sam Brown belts and other equipment so he got quite a head start on us. We can keep up with him
but can't quite overtake him.

This must have made quite a picture: two officers in full uniform
running down the median of the freeway chasing a naked man in a
cowboy hat and boots.

And you will be mighty mistaken if you think the drama ended
there. We had run probably a quarter of a mile when I noticed a
bright orange jeep on the opposite side of the freeway. It pulled
off onto the shoulder ahead of us and stopped. An elderly lady
exited the jeep, walked into the middle of the median strip and
yelled at the naked man who was heading directly towards her.

"You stop right there, young man."

To my utter amazement, he did as she ordered then stood listening as she proceeded to scold him soundly as if speaking to a
naughty child. She ended by saying,

"You sit right down now and wait for those nice police officers."

Again, he obeyed her and sat on the grass waiting for us to catch
up. Without another word, the little old lady got back into her
jeep and drove away.

We were both out of breath when we reached the man but we
took him into custody without further incident, walked him

back to the parked units and turned him over to the Highway Patrol officers who were having trouble keeping straight faces.

"We'll meet you guys over at Emergency and give you a supp report," I growled, the look on my face daring them to say a single word.

Our suspect reeked of alcohol but it was apparent he may have taken some drugs, as well. They won't be able to book him into the jail until they get a clearance from a doctor.

By the time we cleared that call, we were actually on overtime. When we returned to headquarters, gratefully, most of our team had already left for the day. I am, however, dreading what we will face tomorrow.

Sure as God made little green apples, this entire episode will be on the news tonight. I can only imagine what McDoud and I will face at the hands of our fellow "buddies" when we return to work.

Maybe I'll call in sick.

❖ ❖ ❖

CHAPTER ELEVEN

HELPING THE NARCS

I had just stepped out of the shower and was wrapping a towel around my wet head when I heard the doorbell. A glance at my watch, which is on the bathroom counter confirms it is way too early for visitors. Going to the door, I call out,

"Who's there, and what do you want? And it had better be good I mumble under my breath.

"Morrissey, Narcotics," comes the gruff but brief reply.

"You'll have to wait a few minutes while I get decent."

"Take your time, I've got all day."

Who is this smart, Alec?

I'm talking to myself and that's not good. Next thing you know, I'll be getting answers.

My Mom always said,

"Sometimes talking to yourself is the only way to have an intelligent conversation but when you start getting answers start worrying."

I hurriedly jump into a pair of sweats, tuck my "snub nose" into the waistband of my pants and return to the door. I only know Morrissey by reputation and though we work for the same department, I've never met the man. This in itself is not unusual, since a lot of the Narcs are recruited right out of the Academy. You know, new faces and all.

Leaving the safety chain intact, I open the door. Through the small space, I can see a very scruffy looking individual with long hair, an untrimmed beard and an earring in his nostril.

"I need to see some ID."

He passes his badge folder through the opening. I flip it open and study the clean-cut face staring back at me. Mitchell Morrissey is the name that appears on the card inside.

"You're trying to tell me this is your photograph?" I almost laugh out loud. "Wait right there."

I reach into the pocket of my sweats and extract my phone. A quick call to the Department verifies Morrissey's identity.

"Next time call first so you won't have to cool your heels on the porch. This is my day off; this is my private space and I'm not exactly what you'd call fit to receive company."

Still grumbling I escorted him into the living room and sat down.

"Have a seat and tell me what this is all about."

He apologizes for not notifying me then explains the purpose of his visit. It seems some of my neighbors in the small apartment building next door may be drug dealers. Since the apartment in question is located towards the rear of the building it has been difficult for officers to successfully observe any of the suspects' activities. As it so happens that apartment is clearly visible from my kitchen and back porch. The Narcs want permission to do their observing from my home. I can hardly refuse.

So, for the next three days I have to work around detectives perched in my kitchen or on my porch. That apartment is under heavy surveillance, twenty-four, seven but the tenants still manage to pack up and slip out sometime during the third night.

Well, I am sorry those detectives spent so much time on this, only to come up empty-handed but that's the way things happen sometimes.

Two days after those tenants moved out, I start smelling a foul odor coming from the rear of the apartment building. It is so overpowering I have difficulty being out in my back yard. It is definitely the smell of rotting flesh. I finally peek over the fence. To my horror I can see what looks like a grave. Someone has dug a hole and buried something. There is a fresh mound of earth approximately six feet long and four feet wide.

I hurriedly contact Morrissey and he races over. After inspecting the area from over the fence, he contacts Homicide. In no time at all, detectives are all over the place.They start digging, almost afraid of what they might find, considering the caliber of the former occupants.

After two hours of careful excavation, they unearth what is probably the consequence of failing to pay one's electric bill. The "body" turns out to be a couple hundred pounds of freezer-wrapped rotten meat. It has been buried only two feet below the surface: not deep enough to prevent the odor from leaching through.

Morrissey and I feel pretty foolish and the Homicide people don't cut us any slack despite the fact they assure us it is better to be safe than sorry.

The story spreads like wildfire and I am grateful I'm scheduled for remedial training for the rest of the week. Morrissey is left to face the music alone. However, if I thought my being away at training would save me, I was most decidedly WRONG! Those guys in Homicide must have long memories.

When I return to work, I see one of our more artistic brethren has sketched a cartoon on the blackboard in the briefing room. It is of a female officer, wielding a shovel, standing waist deep in a hole with onion peels and fish skeletons flying through the air. Morrissey got off scot free.

The artwork is not signed but I ferreted out the culprit and he paid the price. A week later, when he returned from days off, he found his locker filled to the brim with freshly popped corn. Wonder how that happened?

◆ ◆ ◆

CHAPTER TWELVE

JULY MUD

My God, it's hot! Our cars are air-conditioned but you can't hear much of what's going on outside with the windows rolled up, so one does not reap the full benefit of the cool air.

Angel and I are in separate units but working the same end of the beat today. There has been a rash of daylight burglaries and the "Dicks" have pretty well narrowed it down to the same parolee. We know who he is but finding him is a whole different matter. He has been "at large" for the past three months, and his Parole Officer already has a warrant issued for him. He's been known to frequent our part of town, ergo the concentration in this area.

We're both working the Evening Watch (two p.m. to midnight). We have been canvassing this area, off and on all night, in between calls, with no results.

"You game to make one more sweep before we head for the barn?" asks Angel.

"Sure, why not."

Well, wouldn't you know it? We round a corner and there he is, bold as brass, leaning against a light pole in front of one of the local billiard parlors. He is visiting with four or five other low-life types and the minute they spot us they scatter like flies.

Our guy takes off down the street then cuts across one of the city parks. Now, this is not one of your well maintained, well manicured, up-town sort of parks and the grass hasn't been mowed in perhaps two months.

I jump out of the car and take off after him. Angel yells at me,

"I'll try to head him off at the other end of the park," and he drives off.

The suspect has a little bit of a head start on me but I am having no trouble keeping him in sight. In spite of the disadvantage of the heavy Sam Brown belt I am gaining on him.

I am running as fast as I am able and concentrating on my fleeing suspect when all of a sudden I trip over something hidden in the grass and before I can do anything to stop myself, I go sprawling headfirst and face down into the stickiest, muddiest puddle in the whole world.

"How can there be a mud puddle in this park on one of the hottest days in the middle of July? I'll bet there isn't another mud puddle in the entire city.

"Why here and now?" I literally screamed out loud.

Later investigation will uncover a broken sprinkler that must have been leaking for months because the area immediately around it is saturated and the mud is at least four inches deep.

Trying my best to ignore a ruined uniform, a mud-splattered face and my totally destroyed personal pride, I spring back on my feet and continue the chase. I can still see my suspect; I really haven't lost much ground. The truth is if he had kept right on running he might have gotten away, but he chose to try and hide instead.

I see him dash behind the public bathroom building so I run around the other way to head him off. I am just in time to see him scamper up a tree and jump onto the roof of the small building.

With my flashlight trained on him and my weapon in the other hand, I order him down.

Angel comes running up about then. He looks at me with questions in his eyes but knows better than to say a single word.

Our suspect isn't that bright. He climbs down from his perch as directed but as Angel is slapping the cuffs around his wrists, he looks at me and spits out,

"Hey, pig, you get caught in the rain, or what?"

I have to admit the temptation to make him pay for that remark did cross my mind but what's the point? It isn't as if it will teach him anything. Besides, if we're lucky they'll slap a "violation of parole" on him and we won't have to deal with the likes of him out here on the beat for a long time.

Angel, being the angel he is, transports the prisoner and volunteers to do the reports.

"You head for the barn and get cleaned up then meet me in the report room. A short 'supp' report ought to do it for you."

"Thanks partner. I'll fill you in later, okay?"

"Right."

In the locker room, I wash my face, pick the grass and weeds out of my hair and stuff my soiled uniform into a laundry bag. By the time I jump into a pair of jeans and a T-shirt and go to meet Angel, I hope I look a bit more presentable.

As I walk into the report room, I say,

"Lately, every time I am involved in a foot pursuit, I end up paying the penalty. What's up with that?"

Angel starts to chuckle, "Leave it to you to find the only mud puddle in the entire city in the middle of July."

After a short pause, he adds,

"That's okay, I hear mud packs are good for the complexion."

He ducks just in time to keep from being beaned with my ticket book.

◆ ◆ ◆

CHAPTER THIRTEEN

A HAIRY ASSAULT

J an Wyatt had very long hair so putting it up to comply with on duty safety regulations and still maintain some semblance of style had always been a real challenge. She once told me,

"I always felt like an old woman if I just wound it into a knot at the back of my head," she explained, "then mom gave me an idea. I went out and purchased a false braid. I'd pull my hair into a knot a little higher at the back of my head then secure the braid around it. It made fixing my hair easier and it looked a little more chic as well."

Jan and I were "swapping lies" at the local pizza joint one night after work when she started laughing.

"You'll never believe what happened tonight in Booking. The Feds brought in a drunk biker chick who was screaming and cussing and not cooperating with anybody. We were all "pigs" and she was going to screw us over if she saw us on the street. You know the type."

"Yeah, I've run into a few."

"Anyway," Jan continued, "they had to hold onto her so I could pat her down. Well, she was as big as either of the two guys and very hard to hang onto. While I was checking her crouch area, she tried to kick me then she said with a sneer,

'Is that how you get your kicks, pig?'"

"Well anyway about that time one of the Feds must have loosened his grip a little because she jerked free, came at me with both hands and grabbed for my hair. The trouble is she got a hold of that false braid I told you about and yanked. Well, the damned thing came off in her hands and you should have seen the look on her face. While she was standing there stunned with my 'hair,' in her hands the two Feds and one of the other booking officers dumped her on the floor and cuffed her before she knew what happened. I'll bet she is still wondering what the heck happened."

"All of us were laughing so hard I got a stomachache. That gal still had a glazed look on her face as we marched her off to a security cell."

I was in stitches too listening to Jan's account of the incident. I raised my glass of root beer in a toast.

"Here's to life in the fast lane."

Jan responded with, "You know that old saying, 'what goes around comes around.' Oh yeah!"

Jan and I clicked glasses then busted out laughing again. The other patrons probably thought we were both nuts and maybe drunk.

◆ ◆ ◆

CHAPTER FOURTEEN

MR. CLEAN AND THE GOLDEN SHOWER

Teaching some new recruits that a neatly groomed appearance is as much a part of "good policing" as writing tickets isn't always easy. Somehow it seems to come a lot easier if the recruit is ex-military. "Spit and polish," however, like most anything else can be taken to extreme. Take for instance this experience Jan Wyatt described to me one evening at the local watering hole.

I arrived first, ordered up a pitcher of beer and two glasses and plunked myself down at a table facing the door. We'd had a busy night and I was bushed. I had almost cancelled our monthly after-work get together in favor of a hot shower, and an early-to-bed. Jan and I don't get to "socialize" much and I really do enjoy visiting with her so I flipped a coin. Beer and pizza at Uncle Geno's won out. Now that I'm here I'm glad it did.

I was just pouring my first glass when I saw Jan walk in and bee line it right for our favorite table. I filled her glass and reached up for a quick "high five." When she sat down, she had a peculiar smile on her face.

"Okay, out with it, what now?"

She took a long drink from her glass, looked at me and started shaking her head.

"I thought I had seen everything," she replied. "But what happened tonight takes the cake."

It seems there is a middle aged prostitute who is a "regular" at the jail. Jonnie-Mae is an alcoholic and plies her trade among the old winos down on skid row. It is said she charges only fifty to seventy-five cents and once during the booking process was found to have in her possession a sock full of quarters.

"Tonight they brought in Jonnie-Mae, again. She was really wasted and raving about her dead parents. For her own safety we put her in one of the security cells."

Jan took another sip from her glass, then continued.

"Well, we had a pretty busy night but I checked on her at least once every half hour. She's never violent and when she's sober, she's no trouble at all."

"Anyway, on my last check, I was shocked to find she had taken off all her clothes and climbed the bars all the way to the ceiling. When I tried to talk her down, she refused saying she was trying to talk to her parents and she was closer to Heaven up there. No amount of coaxing would work. I called Control and asked for assistance. If she fell she would crack her skull wide open on the concrete floor."

Jan started to giggle and took another sip.

"Imagine my surprise when the officer that arrived to help was 'Mr. Clean' himself."

"Who's Mr. Clean?"

Jan proceeded to explain. It seems the officer they all called Mr. Clean was new. His shoes were always spit-shined, pants and shirt perfectly creased and every hair in place. He did not like working in the jail and didn't want to touch the inmates. It seems he carried cleanliness to extreme and was very difficult to work with. He also appeared to have a bit of a superiority complex.

"So you see why I was not happy to see him. Anyway, I needed help so I gave him a rundown on the situation and started to tell him what I wanted to do."

"I'll handle this," was his reply, and he told me to open the cell.

"I tried to tell him he should stand by and let me deal with Jonnie-Mae, but he kept insisting he was going to handle things. Well I opened the cell as he insisted and he went into the cell to talk the inmate down."

"Mr. Clean looked up at Jonnie Mae and ordered her to come down. She replied that she couldn't hear him and needed him to come closer. He moved closer and repeated his order. Again she said she couldn't hear and he stepped even closer. Now I was suspicious of her actions but could not have predicted what happened next. Jonnie-Mae swung one leg out from the bars and proceeded to urinate all over Mr. Clean. I can still hear her laughing. He stormed out of that cell and ordered me to let him out of the unit. I let him out then immediately called for more help. Two more officers came up and we were able to drag Jonnie-Mae down from the bars without further incident. We had to secure her with leg irons to keep her from climbing up again. Once she's sober she'll be fine."

"Mr. Clean went down to the Captain's office, signed out and left the building."

By the time Jan finished her story I was laughing so hard I almost choked on my beer.

The following month when we met again for our tete-a-tete, Jan had an update on the Mr. Clean story. It seems he not only left the building that night he marched down to Personnel the following day and resigned from the Sheriff's Department. Perhaps it was just as well. He needed to find another profession. She never did identify the officer by his true name and I never asked. I didn't need to know.

❖ ❖ ❖

CHAPTER FIFTEEN

TAKING AIM

Department regulations require all officers perform weapons qualifications three times a year --- regardless of seniority or time in service. Most of the senior officers feel it is a waste of time.

"I have over ten years on the job. If I don't know how to shoot by now, I better find another job," many "old-timers" have been heard to say.

I have to admit I agree with them but it is a requirement so we all have to comply.

Angel and I have the same beat, the same shift and the same days off so we usually qualify together as well. We'd arrange to meet at the range in uniform about an hour before going on duty.

For some reason I had been dragging my feet lately. In fact, this time I had put it off so long (while making any number of "logical" excuses) that one afternoon as I was going off duty I realized I was running short of time. It boiled down to "do it today or get written up." Actually Angel had been bugging me about it for over a week and he finally gave up on me and went over and took care of his.

I knew the range would be closed by the time I left the office and drove over there so I called ahead to beg a little extra time. I must have caught the Range Master on a good day because he agreed to wait for me and didn't even sound off with a lecture on the last-minute nature of my request.

I hurried to finish changing into my "civies," grabbed up my duty weapon (I carried a revolver in those days), raced out to my car and hurried off to the range. I was walking into the range office when I realized I hadn't brought my Sam Brown belt.

"Damn it, Sully, I forgot my belt. You got an extra I can use?"

"Nah, but that's okay. We'll wing it. When you need to reload I'll hand you the shells."

So saying he locked up the office and followed me down to the target area.

Rick Sullivan (Sully) had been Range Master for eight years. He had been in our department for almost eighteen years and was a member of our pistol team. Sully was fond of saying he chose to work the range because he was getting too old to outrun the bullets in the field. In the opinions of most of his fellow officers there was probably little or nothing about weaponry he didn't know so this assignment was the perfect fit.

The range is not very large considering the size of the department but it is well maintained. It is set up in a recessed earth bowl with high dirt levees on all four sides. Twelve targets are set up at one end and asphalt paved lanes crisscross the manicured lawn at pre-measured distances.

The shoot was moving along smoothly and just when I thought, "great, one more chore out of the way," it happened.

As I reached my hand out to Sully for the last set of reloads, one shell fell from my hand. I quickly bent forward to retrieve it but as it hit the ground it detonated. Shrapnel from that exploding round (a piece of shell casing or lead) struck me in the face on the rim of my eye socket then ricocheted off my closed eyelid.

Needless to say there was blood everywhere as the object tore open the flesh at both sites. Strangely I felt no pain but I was immediately unable to open either eye. Sully took me by the hand and led me back to the office. He grabbed up his squad car keys, called dispatch to report a "code three" transport, rushed me out to the car, and headed for the hospital. Somewhere en route I managed to squeeze open a tiny slit of the uninjured eye but what I saw made me close it tightly again. Trees and telephone poles were whizzing by so fast they were difficult to identify.

I did luck out at the Emergency Room as the on duty physician happened to be one of the staff Plastic Surgeons. He was also originally from Jamaica and had the most fluid and soothing voice. He kept up a running explanation of everything he was doing during his treatment of my injuries and long after I had healed I could still hear that amazing Jamaican accent.

I never got to actually see the doctor that day but I did get to meet him later when I went back for my follow-up exam. I was off duty for a week then "light assignment" for another two weeks. My injuries left no clearly discernable scars thanks to that amazing doctor.

Of course, Angel had to interject his two bits regarding this incident but he delayed his harassment until he was sure I wasn't seriously hurt. I also made the mistake of telling him about the Jamaican doctor. Once I fully recovered and reported for my first regular shift, I found a flower festooned shaggy straw hat hanging on my locker door. Attached was a note saying, "A little something for your trip."

Less than two weeks after my incident another accidental misfire occurred at the range. The circumstances were almost identical: a shell was dropped by an officer. It detonated but this time shrapnel penetrated the officer's pants leg and there was no injury.

Our Chief ordered a thorough investigation. When the accidents were investigated and analyzed they created more questions than answers. Everyone was puzzled. All handgun ammunition in our department is center-fire, so dropping a round on a flat surface should not have detonated it. Further, the waist high fall from a hand to the asphalt below should not have generated sufficient velocity to detonate even if it had been a rim-fire round. What's more, because bullets are made of lead, logically the shell should have fallen "point" down.

Inspections of the asphalt lanes revealed the surfaces were eroded to the point that small bits of gravel were exposed. As improbable as it may seem the inspection team came to the only logical assumption: that the rounds had in fact landed so perfectly they were detonated by the pieces of exposed gravel in the asphalt. Although this could not be unconditionally proven, the Chief ordered the range closed and all the asphalt lanes be replaced by concrete.

No, the team's conclusions were never satisfactorily proven but since the range was renovated, there has not been a repeat of those incidents.

Note: I am still trying to think of a way to repay Angel for his kind gift. It may take a while but I will have my revenge.

◆ ◆ ◆

CHAPTER SIXTEEN

TIGER BY THE TAIL

During my years as a street cop (and there are quite a few) I have to admit to welcoming an occasional dull, boring duty shift but only if there was a guarantee it would stay that way the entire shift. In our line of work things often seem slow and easy then in an instant everything shifts into over drive. I read in a medical journal this was one of the reasons, so many peace officers developed heart issues. The body has trouble dealing with the sudden surges of adrenalin; zero to race in seconds, so to speak.

Tonight's shift was almost over and it had been the ideal: busy enough to make the time move along but not so busy as to leave us with unfinished reports. I say "us" because I'm not riding alone tonight. Angel is riding "shotgun."

I looked over at my partner and commented on the relatively uneventful shift. The words were hardly out of my mouth when the radio began to squawk and the dispatcher's voice broke in,

"Four Charles six."

Giving me an accusatory glare that silently said, "you had to open your big mouth," Angel picked up the mic and responded,

"Four Charles six, go ahead."

We could almost picture the disbelieving grin on the dispatcher's face as she said,

"Four Charles six, proceed to Trinity Street and Main Highway. Driver reports a multi vehicle accident and a tiger in the middle of Main Highway."

Angel almost choked on the candy bar he was munching and said,

"Dispatch, please repeat."

"Four Charles six, I repeat. Proceed to Trinity Street and Main Highway. Driver reports a multi-vehicle accident and a tiger in the middle of Main Highway."

To the dispatcher, Angel said,

"Four Charles six en route. Check."

After securing the mic, he said to me with a lop-sided grin,

"Wonder what kind of hooch that guy got hold of."

I flipped on the lights and siren, made a U-turn and headed in the direction of Main Highway, one of the major expressways through the city. We were less than five minutes away.

En route, Angel contacted dispatch for verification and was told five more citizens had called in with the same report. Now we are no longer laughing. We still aren't believing but no longer laughing. Something is screwy.

We arrive at the Trinity Street on-ramp, slow to a crawl and cautiously enter the expressway. I am sure other emergency vehicles are on the way but it's evident we are the first to arrive. The scene is chaos. At least four-passenger vehicles are crossways in the road and at least two of them look pretty banged up. A large, four door pickup is at least 20 feet further down the road and facing the wrong way in the fast lane. Traffic is at a standstill and some people are standing on the roofs of their vehicles. As soon as the squad unit comes into view those on the roofs start yelling and pointing

I have to drive on the road shoulder to get past but when I do my blood runs cold at what I see and the hair at the back of my neck stands straight up. I hear Angel as he sucks in his breath,

"Geeze!!"

There across the middle lane of this three-lane road, appearing to be taking a nap, is the largest Bengal Tiger I have ever seen. Off-hand I would guess maybe 250 pounds or more.

Angel and I exchange a long look and reaching for the shotguns, slowly open our doors and exit the unit. The walk towards where that cat lay seemed for all the world as if we were partaking in a safari hunt. My heart was pounding so loudly, I was certain it was going to wake that cat. We crept slowly forward expecting the beast to waken any minute, come roaring at us and devour us both -- flesh, bones and all.

Well I began to think that tiger must have had an exhausting night because there wasn't the slightest response from it despite the noises all around us. None the less, my eyes never wavered. They were glued to the body of that beast, watching every muscle for any movement. Just before we reached the animal, I heard a voice shout out,

"I think it's dead. It hasn't moved."

After hearing that I focused my eyes on the cat's midsection. I could see no evidence of breathing but I was not taking anything for granted. I looked at Angel and we nodded to one another. Pointing our shotguns towards the animal we continued forward. When we were within reach, I prodded the cat's head with the barrel of my shotgun. Nothing happened. As I did it again, I heard a female voice call out,

"Oh, please don't shoot him."

We looked up and saw a woman running towards us from the direction of the pickup.

When the woman reached us she explained. Her story was almost as bizarre as the one Angel and I had made up in our minds.

It seems there is a wildlife preserve just west of town. This tiger, which was indeed quite dead, had been living at the preserve for many years. It had suddenly died the day before. Having no idea what caused its death, staff members loaded it into a truck and were taking it to a laboratory for an autopsy. In the process of entering the expressway they got into an accident and the cat's body was thrown onto the roadway, blocking traffic and causing two additional collisions.

As we were speaking with this lady, two back up units arrived as did the Fire Department, two tow trucks and of course, members of the local media. The vehicle that had been carrying the dead tiger seemed to be the least damaged. We assisted in loading the animal back into it.

It required over an hour to collect all the necessary information, try to determine the facts of the circumstances, and make copious notes as my old FTO used to advise. There was a total of five vehicles involved in the accident but no significant damage and no injuries. However, this entire incident more than made up for the previously quiet shift. In fact, by the time we clocked out that night we had invested over two hours in overtime.

Wow! If that isn't the story of a lifetime to tell my kids (if I ever have any). Actually, I may have some trouble convincing them it isn't a fairy tale. I know if it weren't for the witness of the two back up units, Angel and I would have trouble convincing our fellow officers as well. Memories of certain past pranks make me cringe at imagining the potential consequences.

The local news reporters had a field day with this. There was a picture on the front page of the local scandal sheet showing Angel and I pointing our shotguns at the dead tiger and some amusing comments about big game hunters.

I cut out the picture and saved it -- why not?

◆ ◆ ◆

DEDICATION

I am dedicating this book to my law enforcement "family" at large and specifically to those members of my immediate family who are serving or have served faithfully as peace officers. I am indicating my relationship to my fellow officers.

Sgt. Richard Helbush, cousin, deceased, Lake County, CA. Sheriff's Department, killed in the line of duty, May 2, 1981.

CPO Theodore Moss, Sr., father, deceased, US Navy Shore Patrol, died in active service, March 1955.

Ofcr. Theodore Moss, Jr., brother, Ret., Concord, CA. Police Department and Command Sgt. Maj. National Guard Security.

Ofcr. Marta-Bella Bauer, Ret., daughter, Sacramento, CA. Police Department.

Assoc. Warden Ty Sequira, Ret., nephew, California Dept. of Corrections.

Deputy Deborah Morris Hidgon, niece, Alameda County, CA. Sheriff's Department.

FI Timothy Sardelich, foster son, Sacramento, CA. Police Department, Forensic Investigations.

Dep. Thomas Rayzor, Cousin, Amador County, CA. Sheriff's Department.

Ofcr. Glenn Emberson, Ret., grandfather-in-law, deceased, CA. Department of Corrections.

Ofcr. Donald Helbush, Ret., cousin, deceased, Chief Probation, San Mateo County, CA.

Ofcr. Tara Sallizoni, cousin, daughter of Sgt. Richard Helbush, Petaluma, CA. Police Department.

Ofcr. Kalani Schutte, Ret., cousin, deceased, Honolulu, HI. Police Department.

Nanette Anderson, Ret., niece, Associate Governmental Program Analyst, California Highway Patrol.

CSI Maile-Rochet Bauer Reason, granddaughter, Sacramento, CA. Police Department.

Ofc. Nathaniel Reason, grandson-in-law, Sacramento, CA. Police Department.

Khazei-Marin Bauer Geer, granddaughter, Sacramento County, CA. Child Protective Services.

FTO Ofc. Chad Geer, grandson-in-law, Sacramento, CA. Police Department.

Dep. Richard Ditlevsen, husband, Yolo County, CA. Sheriff's Department.

◆ ◆ ◆

ABOUT THE AUTHOR

Patricia Rayzor Ditlevsen

Patricia Rayzor Ditlevsen was born and raised in our 50th State, Hawai'i. Her parents moved the family to the "Mainland" during her last year in high school. Pat had the opportunity to travel around the United States and has lived in or visited twenty-seven states, finally settling in Sacramento, California, with her children. She has always enjoyed creative writing, but the responsibilities of single parenthood made it nearly impossible for her to pursue this pleasure. She became a law enforcement officer in the early sixties and proudly wore the badge for twenty-six years. She retired in 1992. Now she not only has the time to write, but she can draw on past experiences for her stories.

CALL TO ACTION

Finally, please take a moment to review "Another Night on the City Streets." I will appreciate all feedback.

This self-published book was produced and formatted by Gloria Moraga, gloriamorga.com.

Made in the USA
Monee, IL
27 June 2021